≠
E
D388i

I'M TELLING YOU NOW

by Judy Delton • illustrated by Lillian Hoban

E. P. DUTTON • NEW YORK

Library of Congress Cataloging in Publication Data
Delton, Judy.   I'm telling you now.
Summary: Artie discovers there are many things he is not
supposed to do, but always after the deed has been done.
[1. Behavior—Fiction]   I. Hoban, Lillian, ill.   II. Title.
PZ7.D388Im   1983   [E]   82-17714
ISBN 0-525-44037-2

Published in the United States by E. P. Dutton, Inc.,
2 Park Avenue, New York, N.Y. 10016
Editor: Ann Durell   Designer: Claire Counihan
Printed and bound in Hong Kong
by South China Printing Co.
First Edition   10 9 8 7 6 5 4 3

for Beverly Vavoulis,
who, like Charlotte, is in a class by herself
a true friend and a good writer

"Don't cross the street, Artie," said my mother as I went out the back door to play.

"I won't," I said. "I never cross the street."

"Good," said my mother.

I sat on the back steps and thought about what to do. I saw a ladder leaning against the Perkins' house. It reached way up to the roof.

"I wonder what's up there," I said.

I went over to look at the ladder. I put my foot on the first step. Before long, I was at the top.

I stepped onto the roof. Looking down, I could see the post office. I could see Mr. Rogers walking his dog, Champ. I saw my mother hanging sheets on the clothesline.

"Hi Mom," I called.

"Artie?" said my mother. She shaded her eyes and looked around.

"Up here," I called.

"Arthur Ray!" she said. "You get down from there this minute."

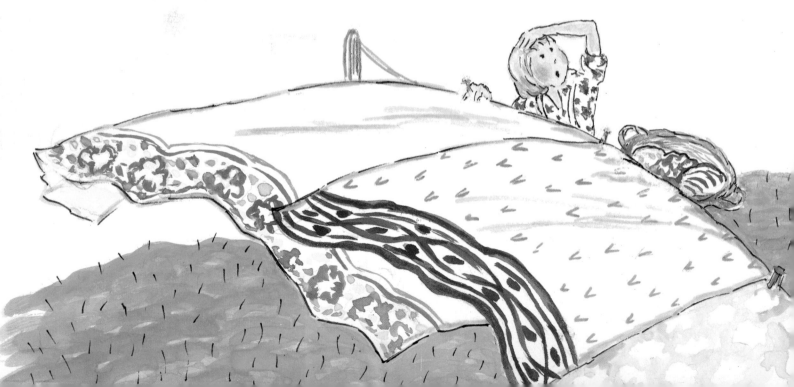

When I got down, my mother was cross.

"You never told me not to climb up ladders," I said.

"Well, I'm telling you now," she said.

The next morning when I went out to play, my mother said, "Artie, don't cross the street, and don't climb any ladders."

"All right," I said. I sat on the steps and tried to think of something to do. I watched the cars go by. Some of them stopped at the Johnsons' house next door. People with little kids got out. They went into the Johnsons' back yard.

"I wonder what's going on," I said. I decided to find out.

When I got there, Mrs. Johnson was passing out paper hats to the little kids.

"Why, hello, Artie!" she said. "We're having a birthday party for Ricky."

"I'll help," I said.

She gave me some balloons to hand out.

After that we played games, and I gave out the prizes.

When it was time to eat, we had hot dogs and birthday cake. We sang "Happy Birthday."

I stayed to clean up the yard.

"Artie!" I heard my mother call. "Lunchtime."

"I had lunch," I said when I got home.

"Where?" she said.

"At the party," I said.

"What party?" she said. "You weren't invited to a party."

"Invited?" I said.

"Arthur Ray, you don't go to places where you're not invited!"

"You never told me that before," I said.

"I'm telling you now," said my mom.

The next morning I got dressed and ate breakfast
and went out in the back yard.

"Artie," said my mom. "Don't cross the street,
and don't climb ladders, and don't go to any parties."

"I won't," I said.

I sat down on the back steps and watched the
breeze blow the treetops. It skipped along right
over the leaves.

"I'd like to skip," I said.

I took my jump rope and skipped along the sidewalk. When I got to the drugstore, there was a dog tied to the tree outside. The dog was whimpering.

"What's the matter, boy?" I said to the dog.

He was pulling at his leash as if he wanted to get away. All of a sudden, the leash came loose. I grabbed it. The dog jumped up and licked me.

"I'll bet you want a little walk," I said. He did.

When we started to walk, his tail started to wag. He didn't whimper anymore.

When we passed my house, my mother was typing on the front porch.

"Arthur Ray, whose dog is that?" she said.

"I don't know," I said.

"Where did you get it?" she said.

"Next to the drugstore," I said.

"Take that dog back where you found him as fast as you can, and don't ever take any dogs again."

"You never told me not to," I said.

"Well, I'm telling you now," said my mother.

The next morning I went outside and sat on my back steps. I watched a man digging a hole. He was fixing the street.

"I'd like to dig a hole in the empty lot down the street!" I said. "A deep, deep hole all the way through the earth to China."

I was on my way to find a shovel when I
remembered something. "I'll bet my mother
wouldn't like it if I dug a hole through the earth
and came out the other end and lived in China.
I better ask her," I said.

My mom was making raspberry jam in the
kitchen.

"Can I dig a hole in the empty lot all the way through the earth to China?" I said.

"Why, of course, Artie. Why in the world couldn't you dig a hole in the empty lot down the street?"

"You never told me I could," I said.

My mom wiped her hands on her apron and gave me a hug.

"Well, I'm telling you now," said my mother.